MELT DOWN MURDER

SUNDAE AFTERNOON COZY MYSTERIES, BOOK 2

GRETCHEN ALLEN

SUMMER PRESCOTT BOOKS PUBLISHING

CHAPTER ONE

Yvette Lockhart met her friend, Gavin Dillinger, on the shared front porch of their duplex.

"I brought out some lemonade in case you change your mind." Yvette pointed to the tray she'd set down on the table.

"Thanks. I might need it after all. It's hotter than I thought it was going to be out here today," he swiped a rag across his forehead. Although it was summer, the heatwave the little New England town of Heritage, Massachusetts was experiencing was out of the ordinary for this time of year.

Yvette made sure Gavin had stuck to his end of the deal after he'd surprised her with a last-minute catering gig for a party his girlfriend was having. So, today, he was repainting both of their front doors, setting up some hanging plants, and clearing the mulch beds around the sides of the house.

"I just checked the weather app on my phone. It says the heat index is up to over a hundred degrees," Yvette called over her shoulder as she trotted down the three steps to their brick walkway that led to the street. "Want me to grab your mail?"

"Sure, thanks." Gavin made his way around to Yvette's side of the porch, reaching up with both arms to hang a stunning, scarlet ivy geranium.

Geraniums were always one of Yvette's favorites. Thinking back to when she was young, her grandmother would take her to the local nursery to pick out flowers. Every week, they'd deliver a bouquet to a stranger they met on the street, hoping to offer them a little bit of kindness. She'd actually considered starting something like that again, knowing everyone could use a bit of unexpected kindness in their lives. Snapping out of her daydream, Yvette pulled the mail from both of their boxes and headed back up to the house. "Break time already?" She laughed, seeing Gavin leaning against the wooden porch column.

"Ha. Ha. I've done everything you asked. I think I deserve it."

Yvette inspected his handiwork. "Everything

looks amazing. You know how I love to repaint the doors."

"You mean, you love when I repaint the doors..."

Several times a year, based on what season it was or what mood she was in, Yvette would drag her best friend, Amelia, to the hardware store to look for paint. They'd always meet for lunch at Carlisle's Bistro, stop at the hardware store, and then spend an hour poring over the color options before finally deciding. Then she'd go home and talk Gavin into painting their doors. This time, she'd chosen a cool turquoise, thinking it would be a perfect color to end the summer with.

"They look amazing!" Yvette clapped her hands together. "We shouldn't have to change them again until fall."

Gavin chugged his icy glass of lemonade. "Fall is coming pretty quickly, but at least the weather will have cooled down by then."

"You know how I get when it comes to that time of year. The colors and smells of the season get me every time. And you can't forget the decorations! Have you been to the stores lately? All the fall stuff is out already. The market in Merryville is already set up for Halloween."

"A little early for that, isn't it?" Gavin rolled his eyes.

Yvette shrugged. "If I had it my way, it'd be a perpetual fall, and I'd have a pumpkin latte every morning."

"Of course, you would. I'm partial to summer myself. I like the heat, even if I complain about it." Gavin chuckled.

"It's gonna be even hotter this weekend, but I can't wait to get to the lake house. I don't think anyone has been up there since Mark and Amelia broke up."

"Those two are something else. I never understood what exactly went on with them." Gavin shook his head.

"I'm Amelia's closest friend, and while I have my suspicions, even I don't really know what happened. Other than the fact that Mark can be a colossal jerk sometimes."

"He does have a bit of a dry sense of humor, doesn't he?" Gavin agreed.

The two friends sat quietly for a few moments before noticing a little, green car slowly come to a stop in front of the house. The sweet, newly engaged couple inside had just purchased the tiny ranch-style home next door. Jamie, the future bride, was living there on her own for now, while her fiancé, Evan, was staying at his apartment in the neighboring town of Merryville until after the wedding.

"Hey, you two!" Yvette called out.

"Come sit for a while." Gavin waved them up to the porch.

The young couple got out of their car and held hands as they walked up to the porch.

"Everything looks so pretty." Jamie glanced around at all the changes. "You do such lovely work, Gavin. We might have to borrow you for a few things once we get settled in after the wedding."

"Landlord and handyman extraordinaire." Yvette chuckled. "Better stop doing such a good job before the whole neighborhood tries to hire you."

"Wait, you don't do this for a living?" Jamie attempted to hide her embarrassment.

"Not really. I just try and take care of my properties and tenants."

"Maybe you should consider it," Evan suggested. "It does look pretty great around here. In fact, all your properties do. We've been looking around at places for my mom while she and my aunt are here visiting. She'll be officially moving here within the next couple months, but we've come up with nothing. Every building of yours has a wait list and the only other one we found is being sold. We don't want to get her in there and end up having the new owners tear it down or something."

"You should go check it out, Gavin. Maybe you can buy it," Yvette mused.

Gavin hesitated. "I'm always willing to look, but ever since my dad fully retired from the family business, my plate is pretty full. I recently purchased an apartment building on the outskirts of town and it's going to need quite a bit of work before I can even get anyone in there."

"We understand. If you have any availabilities in the near future, please, keep us in mind," Evan said.

"I'll see what I can do," Gavin promised.

"So, how are things going with you, Yvette?" Jamie asked.

"Really good, actually. I'm taking a girl's trip this weekend with a friend, and the shop is doing great. We've hired a new employee and business is booming. I can't complain about a thing."

Sundae Afternoon, the local ice cream shop Yvette managed, was smack dab in the center of town. Its colorful interior, and reputation for some of the most delicious and decadent frozen treats, drew in more guests than ever. The Heritage location was the only one open year-round, despite the chilly winter months in New England.

"I think we'll stop in soon. I picked up a copy of your paper a few days ago when I was at that little consignment shop downtown. The Malibu mango ice cream sounds to die for," Jamie gushed.

"Oh no! Thanks for reminding me. After everything that happened last week, I completely forgot to switch out the paper at all the local shops." Yvette slouched back in her chair and hung her head.

Once a month, Sundae Afternoon put out a paper newsletter announcing all the newest flavors and offerings from the shop. Typically, Yvette kept over fifty different types of ice cream on hand, and the featured flavors that did exceptionally well stayed on the menu for a bit longer than the others.

"Darn, does that mean I can't get that kind?" Jamie stuck out her bottom lip.

"I think we kept that one, but if not, I'll make sure to order it for the next delivery." Yvette laughed. "I can't believe I forgot. I never do that."

"I don't think anyone will hold it against you," Gavin said, rolling his eyes. "You were just recently involved in a murder investigation…"

"What?!" Evan exclaimed.

"I was not! I only wanted to figure out what

happened is all. I got caught up, wrong place, wrong time."

"Ehhh, I mean, you were convinced that the only real suspect was innocent. You accused someone of murder, and you were there when the actual killer confessed. I think it's safe to say you were pretty involved," Gavin reminded her.

"Are you finished?" Yvette asked, noticing the shocked looks on the young couple's faces. "You're scaring our guests."

"Are you okay? What am I saying? Of course, you're okay, you're sitting right here," Jamie babbled.

Yvette offered a reassuring smile. "I'm fine. Gavin here is making it sound way worse than it was. And it's not like it's going to happen again."

"Let's hope not," Gavin said.

"Well, we'd better get going. We've got plenty of errands to run today," Evan said. "Gavin, you have my number, so if you see any rentals pop up, please don't forget to give me a call."

"Definitely," Gavin agreed, standing, and extending a hand to Evan.

"It was nice to see you guys and thank you both. I'll see you soon for some of that yummy ice cream!" Jamie waved to Yvette before the couple headed back to their vehicle.

CHAPTER TWO

Yvette stood in the doorway of her office, discreetly observing her employees.

"So, it's two scoops of buttercrunch and one Dutch chocolate in the Heritage High Sundae, right?" Max asked Vanessa, his trainer for the day.

Max Woodward had come over from Sundae Afternoon's second location in Connecticut. He was there to learn how things worked in Yvette's shop since he'd be helping out when she was gone for the weekend.

"No, it's two buttercrunch and one maple bacon." Vanessa sighed.

Max nodded. "That makes sense, considering there's bacon on top of the sundae. Although, bacon and chocolate go well together too. Maybe you can try it that way?"

"Every year, the graduating class at Heritage High School votes on what goes in the sundae they have named after them. So, I think it's best that we keep it how it is," Vanessa explained.

Yvette was hoping that having Max around would work out well since the majority of the rules were the same in each of the Sundae Afternoon shops. She figured he'd be able to handle it for the most part, but she knew that Vanessa, no matter how good of a worker she was, sometimes got a little frustrated with people who didn't get things right the first time around.

Noticing Vanessa's forced smile, Yvette came the rest of the way out of her office. "Hey, you two! How's it going?" she asked cheerfully, making her way to the front counter.

"Really good. I think I'm learning a lot, but it's very different over here. Your menu is so much bigger, and you are way busier. Vanessa has to keep stopping to talk to customers. We don't do much of that at our shop. They just order, pay, eat, and leave."

"That's the most important part," Yvette said, tilting her head. "Of course, the ice cream has to taste good, and we work hard to make each order as close to perfect as we possibly can but getting to know the customers has always been our number one priority. We ask every single person who walks through those doors what their name is. We also do our best to learn what they like to order so the next time they come in; they can just ask for their *usual*." Yvette smiled but was cringing on the inside at the thought of what Henry, the manager of the Connecticut shop, was teaching his staff.

"A lot of times, I see a customer pull into the parking lot and I have their order waiting for them when they come in," Vanessa said proudly. "That always gets me the biggest tips."

"You guys get tipped here?" Max's green eyes widened.

"It's not about the money, but yes. Treating the customers like friends is what keeps them coming back, and honestly, a lot of them have become more than friends over the years. We're like a little family here in Heritage."

"Wow. I'm really looking forward to working here. Not only for the money but it sounds like you make working fun. Henry doesn't do that. Maybe when you come work with us at my shop, you can change a few things?" Max looked hopeful.

"How'd you know about that?" Yvette asked.

"Henry told me. Am I not supposed to know? Are you not coming?"

Emma Kline, the owner of Sundae Afternoon, had asked Yvette to work in the Connecticut location for a week when Henry was on vacation. Not only did they need someone to cover for him, but Emma also wanted her to do some investigating as to why the store's sales were dropping. Yvette had a few guesses already and she hadn't even stepped foot in the place.

"Uhh, no. It's okay. I'm coming. I just didn't know anyone knew about it yet."

"We're all nervous. We know how long you've been part of the company and how much Emma loves you, so it's got the whole shop a little freaked out," Max admitted.

Yvette was embarrassed. "I'm only helping out while Henry is on vacation, and I won't be making any changes. It's no big deal."

"Well, either way, I'm glad I get to be here to learn from the best."

The bell on the front door jingled, and two older women walked in. One sat down quickly by the door and the other was headed for the counter. "Why don't you take care of them on your own? Don't forget to ask their names and introduce yourself." Yvette nudged the younger man forward.

"I see where he's coming from, you know." Vanessa turned to face her boss after looking at the woman sitting by the door for a little longer than necessary.

"What are you looking at?" Yvette asked.

"She looks really familiar. I thought it was odd she sat down so quickly and didn't order with her friend but oh well." She dismissed the thought with a wave. "Anyway, you've been working here for a long time and have always been close to Emma and her family."

Yvette crinkled her nose. "That's silly. I'm probably more nervous than they are. I may have been around for a while, but I've only ever worked here or at the farm. I've never gone to another store for anything other than to volunteer for the day during an event or something."

Her trip to the lake was only a couple of days away and she was thankful Max was at the shop to help out. It seemed like things were going well and that her staff would do just fine without her. The lake house was in Heritage, so even if something did come up that they couldn't handle, she wouldn't be too far away. Yvette trusted her team and was going to treat this like a trial run for when she was in Townsend in a couple of weeks. She'd feel much better about leaving, knowing that everything was under control.

Vanessa pressed her finger to her lips. "Look at Max. He's doing so good! It's as if he and

the customer are old pals."

"This may work out better than I expected." Yvette beamed.

She walked over toward the duo as they talked and pulled the order slip from Max's fingers, so he wouldn't have to step away from the conversation.

"Two skillet sundaes. I haven't made one of these for a while!" Yvette exclaimed when she saw the order. "Can you make sure the oven is up to temp?" she asked Vanessa.

"On it!" Vanessa agreed and rushed to the kitchen.

"Excuse the interruption, but I just wanted to let you know that the skillet sundaes take a bit longer to prepare since the cookie is baked to order, is that okay?" Yvette asked the woman talking with Max.

"Absolutely." She nodded. "I'd wait all day for something that sounds as good as that cookie does."

"We'll get them out to you as soon as we can." Yvette grinned and headed for the kitchen.

She pulled out the prepared cookie dough from the walk-in cooler and placed it in a small skillet to be baked. The piping hot, thick and chewy chocolate chip cookies would be topped with mocha pecan ice cream and drenched in hot fudge and whipped cream. There was nothing better than creating something so decadent, and perfecting the presentation of the sundae was one of her favorite things to do. Yvette hoped the customers would enjoy it and that Max would be inspired by her creation.

CHAPTER THREE

Yvette went over her packing list for the final time. After double and triple checking that everything she needed was ready to go, she realized the last thing left on the list she needed was something she'd have to go to her parent's house to pick up. Yvette texted her mom to let her know she'd be stopping by soon and sat back in her recliner, deciding to relax for a few minutes and enjoy her morning coffee. After all, it was barely seven a.m. and she'd already been up for two hours preparing for her weekend getaway.

She couldn't wait to get to the lake house. It may not be the girl's trip she and Amelia had dreamed of, but Lake Winterwater was a perfectly suitable location for the friends to take a few days for themselves. Mark and Amelia had purchased the house together when they were dating, and while they were no longer together, they'd made the choice to keep the house. They rotated weeks, so both could enjoy the home they had renovated themselves.

"Knock, knock." Yvette heard a voice singsong through the open window of her living room.

"You're here early," she said once Amelia let herself in.

The two had been friends for so long, they'd felt comfortable enough to walk into each other's homes without giving it a second thought.

"Weird, right? I'm never early." She laughed at herself.

"Here I was thinking I had all this time to relax," Yvette teased.

"I'm looking forward to this weekend and I couldn't sit still, so I came over hoping you'd be ready too. I haven't been out to the lake yet this summer. I'd expected to get down there a few times, but with work and the trip to see my grandparents, I just haven't had the time. Is that all you're bringing?" Amelia babbled, stopping to gawk at the tiny luggage set by the front door.

"We aren't leaving the state, or even the town for that matter. How much do I really need? We'll either be by the water or around the house the whole time. I did bring a nice outfit for tomorrow night in case we wanted to go out to dinner."

Amelia shrugged. "I brought three bathing suits, a set of pajamas and four outfits. I packed two sundresses too, and I have a separate bag for shoes and one for makeup."

Yvette should have known better than to ask. Her friend always over packed. A couple years ago, the two had taken a week-long trip to Michigan for the National Ice Cream Expo and decided to drive there. Amelia brought along four suitcases, which were all full to the brim, and Yvette wasn't sure that she'd even opened two of them up the entire trip.

"Good thing we're taking my SUV. We'd never have enough room in your little car. Did you bring your things with you, or do we need to stop by your house?" Yvette stood and looked out the window.

"I brought everything. I think we can leave right from here if you don't mind me keeping my car in your driveway."

"Of course, you can. I'll have Gavin keep an eye on it while we're gone." Yvette grabbed her car keys. "I have to run to my parents and grab a cooler. I was going to stop on our way to the lake, but we could get a little bite to eat and bring it back here first. We still have plenty of time to pack up the car before we have to head out."

Amelia tossed her purse over her shoulder and headed out the front door behind her friend. "I saw the sign out at Brews on my way here. They have a spinach and sundried tomato quiche on special today. We should totally get that, and whatever we don't finish we can leave for Gavin."

"That sounds delicious!" Yvette squinted, shading her eyes from the sun. "You parked behind me. Do you just want to take your car?"

"Sure, we can do that but maybe we should take my luggage out first because there's no way one more thing is going to fit in there."

"It's one cooler." Yvette reminded her.

"Trust me. Nothing else will fit."

Yvette shook her head at her friend and opened the door to look inside the car." You weren't joking."

"Told you."

They pulled out the bags from Amelia's tiny car and transferred them into Yvette's much larger and more practical SUV. Eager to get their vacation started, they climbed inside Amelia's car, and headed toward the Lockhart's home on Cottage Street.

CHAPTER FOUR

"The first thing I want to do when we get there is call the shop to make sure everything is okay," Yvette said from the driver's seat an hour or so later.

"No, the first thing we're going to do is sprint to the dock and sit by the water for a while. I don't even want to go into the house beforehand. There's something about sitting out there that calms me. I need calm, we both do. I could have driven if you wanted to spend the whole time checking on work stuff."

"I don't want to spend the whole time doing that. I only wanted to see how things are going. I've never left for more than one day before. I mean, I've gone away, but Emma was always there to take my place."

"Vanessa is more than capable of handling things and like you pointed out to me before, we aren't even leaving town. Nothing that crazy is going to happen and even if it does, you aren't far away. You probably scheduled all the other staff for the entire weekend too so I'm betting everything will be fine." Amelia poked her friend in the arm.

Yvette let out a breath. "You're right. I do want to be on the water, and I do trust Vanessa. I never understand how you don't worry about things. You leave your secretary alone all the time and you're the director of Tourism and Activities for the entire town. You're lucky that nothing bad ever happens."

"To be fair, nothing bad ever happens when you leave either," Amelia teased. "I also don't just 'leave my secretary alone'. I have someone who covers me when I'm gone. Carina comes over from the Senior Center and takes over all the events and tours. Although, I do try to keep the schedule light when I'm traveling."

"Alright, alright. I'll make the one phone call and I won't let it cross my mind again."

"Good, because we only have a couple days at the lake, and I don't want to spend it thinking about work. I'd much rather spend it having a good time with you."

They drove about ten minutes longer before seeing the stunning view of Lake Winterwater to the right of them. The tranquil water, glimmering with sparkles under the heat of the summer sun was a sight for sore eyes. They spotted several boats, and families playing together on the shore. It would be only minutes before they'd arrive at the lake house, and they could join in on the fun, too.

Yvette drove slowly up the road toward the house. It was exactly how she remembered it. The pale-blue exterior of the home was so inviting, and the backdrop boasted some of the most beautiful birch, and white oak trees she had ever seen. The women got out of the vehicle and took in their surroundings quietly before trading a look and running together toward the dock.

"I love it." Amelia sat on the dock with her feet hanging off the edge into the water. "It always feels like a whole new world when I'm here."

Undoing her ponytail and shaking out her wavy, brown hair, Yvette laid down on the gently rocking dock. "Me too. I'm sorry you and Mark didn't get to enjoy it together for longer."

"It is what it is." Amelia shrugged. "I think we're lucky to have a place like this right in our hometown and I'm glad we decided to keep it."

"Do you miss him?" Yvette sat up and looked curiously at her friend.

"Yeah, but I don't really think I have a right to. I'm the one who caused the breakup."

Yvette slipped off her sandals and put her feet into the water. "He's the one who broke up with you."

"Because we didn't seem to want the same things, but now I'm not so sure…" she trailed off, looking into the water.

"I don't understand."

"I miss him, and I think he might have been right. We were perfect for each other and I ruined that when I told him I didn't ever want to get married." Amelia leaned back on her elbows and closed her eyes, letting the warmth of the sun hit her face.

"Well, do you?" Yvette asked, realizing that she'd been right in her assumptions of why their relationship had ended.

"I might," she replied slowly, "but it's probably too late."

Yvette could barely contain her excitement. She knew how much Mark adored Amelia and how great of a match they really were. Her friends deserved happiness and if she had her way, she'd be getting them back together as soon as the weekend was over.

"I think you should talk to him, but right now, all we need to worry about is having fun. No work and no men." Yvette jumped up from her spot, ready to get her vacation started.

Amelia rolled her eyes. "Didn't you say you had to call the shop and check in?"

"Oh, yeah," Yvette snorted and pulled out her phone. "Right after I make this call."

"Can you help me carry some of this stuff?" Amelia blew a wisp of hair out of her eyes.

"Are you kidding? You look ridiculous." Yvette cackled when she saw her friend.

Amelia pulled two suitcases behind her, had a beach bag over each shoulder and her purse around her neck. Her floppy, oversized hat was covering nearly half her face and Yvette was sure she couldn't see where she was going.

"I can't help it. I didn't want to make more than one trip. I'm excited to be here and I'd rather not spend any more time than necessary bringing things inside."

Yvette nudged her friend's hat back to where it belonged and took one suitcase and a bag off of her hands. The girls carried the luggage up the steps and stopped when they reached the front door so Amelia could dig the key out of her pocket.

"I am so ready for this!" Yvette exclaimed as Amelia pushed the front door open.

"Ewww, what is that smell?" Amelia dropped her bags and covered her nose.

"Oh, wow, yeah. It's not very pleasant, whatever it is. It's like a mixture of rotten meat and dirty socks." Yvette did her best not to gag. "How long has this place been closed up?"

Amelia looked around the living room. "I don't know the last time Mark was here, but I haven't been here in about six months or so. Let's open the windows or something and try to air it out a little."

Yvette lifted her shirt over her mouth and nose to block the smell and helped slide some of the windows open on the main floor. "Want me to do the ones upstairs too?" she asked.

"Yeah, that's probably a good idea. I'll be up there in just a minute. I'm going to make sure there's no food in the fridge that accidentally got left in there the last time someone was here."

Yvette knew the house like the back of her hand. Granted it'd been a while since she'd been there herself, but she'd spent several weekends there in the past. Leaving the living room and making a quick right down the hallway, she went up the stairs that led to the loft. She figured she'd start there since that's where she'd be sleeping for the weekend.

Coming face to face with the most horrifying thing she'd ever seen in her life, Yvette let out a blood-curdling scream before turning and running back down the stairs to where Amelia was.

"What the heck is wrong?"

"I... there... oh my gosh," was all she could get out before terror took over.

Amelia rushed to her friend's side just as she dropped to the floor. "What's the matter? Are you okay?"

"We n-need to c-call the police," she managed to say.

"What, why? Is there someone in the house?" Amelia panicked. "We need to get out of here." She tried pulling her friend up.

Yvette's heart raced, and she couldn't convince her trembling body to cooperate. Her eyes welled with tears. "I don't think it matters if we leave or not."

"I'm going up there myself if you won't tell me what's going on right this second. I swear if you saw a bug or something and are freaking out I'm going to kill you."

"No! Don't go up there." Yvette lunged toward her friend and grabbed her by the leg.

"Alright, now you're scaring me."

"Just trust me, you don't want to go up there." Yvette reached forward and took her phone from her purse and dialed the emergency numbers she hoped she'd never have to call. "Let's go outside and wait. I don't want to be in here for a second longer." She forced herself up and took her friend by the arm.

CHAPTER FIVE

"When did you say you arrived?" Deputy Rodney Calhoun asked.

"We got here around nine o'clock or so, but we spent some time out by the water talking for a little bit before we ever even came into the house," Yvette answered, still shaken.

"And you were the one to find the body?"

"Yes. When we walked in, there was a really strong smell, and we were going around opening windows to clear it out. I went upstairs to do those windows and that's when I saw it...him." Her stomach clenched. "I'm sorry. I've never seen something like that before. There was so much blood. I just...I'm sorry," Yvette stuttered.

"I completely understand. Seeing a body is never

pleasant for anyone," the deputy agreed. "I only have a few more questions."

"Of course. I'll do anything I can." Yvette looked around the yard for Amelia. She was talking with Heath Briggs, the chief of police.

"This is your friend's property?

"Yes. She owns it with her ex-boyfriend, Mark Kline."

The deputy raised a brow. "She owns it with her ex? That's unusual."

"I guess. It didn't end on bad terms or anything. They purchased the place when they were still dating and they both loved it so much that they didn't want to give it up, so they kept it."

"I see. You said Mark Kline is his name?"

"Yes, but what does he have to do with this? Oh, no. Do you think it was him up there? I didn't get a good look at his face. I saw all the blood and ran away as fast as I could."

"We're unsure of the identity of the victim right now. That information wouldn't be available until after the family is notified, anyway."

Yvette's breathing started to hitch again, and her mind began to spin. What if it really was Mark up there? After the family is notified... That's Emma. She'd be devastated.

"I have to see my friend." She turned and raced over towards Heath and Amelia.

"Ma'am, I just have a few more questions," the deputy called to her as he followed close behind.

"I'll take care of it, Rodney," Heath told him.

"Yes, sir." The deputy nodded and headed toward the crime scene.

"Girls, I know this is a shock, but I need you to try to hold it together and cooperate with us as best you can."

"I'm sorry, Heath. I can't stand the thought that there's someone dead in my house. Who could it even be? Why were they here? No one even has keys but Mark and me." Amelia's body shivered. "Oh no, Mark…"

"Heath, can we please call Mark?" Yvette asked when she realized Amelia had the same concerns as she did.

"I'm going to have to ask you to not do that. We have someone on their way to see him now. We need to go about this the right way, which doesn't include you two getting involved. I understand you're both worried, but it's best if you let us discuss this with Mark," he answered.

"Okay," they gave each other a look but agreed in unison.

"Yvette, you need to see Deputy Calhoun. I know he has more questions for you," Heath reminded her.

"I just need another minute to compose myself." She sniffled. "I want to offer all the help I can," Yvette assured Heath before taking Amelia by the hand and leading her a few steps away toward the dock.

"I don't think I can wait for someone to tell me if Mark is okay," Amelia said. "I need to call him."

Yvette took the phone from her friend's hand and scanned the area, making sure no one was paying attention to them, and that Heath was far enough away. She dialed Mark's number. "We're going to. We need to know that he's okay."

"You heard Heath, though. He said we couldn't."

"I know but I can't wait either, so we're gonna have to be quick. Even if we only hear his voice when he picks up." Yvette tried to justify that doing what Heath had specifically asked her not to do was okay since they wouldn't be discussing the murder. She hesitated a moment before pressing send.

"Why isn't he picking up?" Amelia swayed on her feet.

"He's probably at work. I'll call the farm." Yvette hung up and dialed again.

When there was no answer on Mark's office line,

Yvette grabbed her friend in a big embrace. "It's okay," she told her as she tucked the phone into Amelia's pocket. "Everything is going to be okay."

"What if it's him up there? What if he's dead? Oh, Yvette, I'm so sorry you had to see something so horrific." Amelia burst into tears.

Yvette was still finding it difficult to breathe and her heart was nearly beating out of her chest, but she had to be strong. She never allowed herself to be overemotional and took pride in how well she handled difficult situations. This may have been more than just a difficult situation, but she refused to let it show that anything was getting to her.

The girls looked up to see Deputy Calhoun heading toward them. "Yvette? We're going to need to finish up now."

"Yes, sir. I'm sorry it took me so long, but I'm ready now."

Yvette gave Amelia's hand one last squeeze before turning to follow the deputy back toward the side of house.

CHAPTER SIX

Yvette's eyes fluttered open. She rolled over to look at her alarm clock and remembered that she'd stayed the night at Amelia's house. She'd planned on going back to bed and was about to draw the blankets back up to her face when she heard a faint cry coming from the next room. She maneuvered her legs off the side of the bed and walked over to the wall. She placed her ear against it and listened for a few moments before deciding she should go check on her friend.

Yvette knocked lightly on Amelia's bedroom door before gently pushing it open. "Are you okay?" she asked.

"I'm not sure. I stayed up almost the whole night calling and texting Mark, but he never responded. I know we aren't in the best place right now, but I know he'd answer if he saw I called that many times."

"We can call Heath in a little while and see if he was able to get in touch with him." Yvette gave her friend an encouraging look.

"I can't stop thinking about it. I go from being sick over the thought that he's dead to being jealous he's not picking up the phone because he's with another woman. I even went so far as to consider that he knew the victim and was in some sort of trouble, so he ran away. Or maybe he even got kidnapped or something. I can't even think straight. Mark would kill me if he knew I was accusing him of murder."

Yvette was trying to hold it together, but truthfully, she was about ready to break down herself. She needed to try to get some food in her stomach since neither of them had eaten since breakfast the morning before. "Why don't we go downstairs for a little while and listen to some music? I'll make us something to eat." She didn't think turning on the television was the right choice when what had happened would no doubt be all over the news.

Amelia gave a halfhearted smile. "I don't know if I have much of an appetite, but I'll sit with you while you cook."

Yvette searched the cabinets and refrigerator until

she found something she could put together that resembled a meal. "I know you said you aren't hungry, and I also know it's eight a.m. but what about some grilled cheese and tomato soup?" She held out a can of soup in one hand and a loaf of sourdough bread in the other.

She shrugged. "I do love comfort food and we could both use a little bit of comforting," Amelia agreed. "Are you sure you don't mind? I'm being such an awful friend. You're the one who saw that awful thing and here I am making you cook for me."

"You know how much I love cooking, plus it calms me down when I'm feeling anxious. Before you know it, your kitchen will be full of casseroles and cupcakes. Oh, cupcakes! We should make cupcakes." Yvette opened the fridge to look for eggs.

"I think grilled cheese and soup will be okay for now." Amelia pulled out a bottle of water from the fridge.

"Fine. But if we still haven't heard from Mark after we're done eating, I say we go talk to Heath at the police station and stop at Sundae Afternoon on our way back. I think we could use some ice cream in our lives."

Yvette finished whipping up their makeshift breakfast and they picked at their food in silence.

They were just about done when a cell phone dinged. Jolted by the noise, both girls jumped and dashed for their respective phones.

"It's mine," Yvette said glancing down at the screen. The color drained from her face. "It's a text from Millie at the farm."

Millie Rutherford worked at Kline Family Farm with Mark, so maybe she had heard from him. Yvette was hopeful that was the case.

"What does it say?" Amelia took a few steps closer and strained to see the text message.

"We're going to have to see Heath sooner rather than later. Millie said she came into work this morning and Mark wasn't there. Then one of the farmhands came by her office and dropped off his cell phone. I guess he found it in the coop when he was gathering eggs."

"It was him. He was the one up there. He was at the lake, and someone broke in and killed him. I just know it." Amelia's face was getting paler by the minute.

"We don't know that. This certainly isn't good news, but we can't be sure of anything yet. Let's get dressed and go find Heath. I bet he has more informa-tion than we do at this point. I don't know what he'll be able to tell us, but it won't hurt to at least ask him a few questions."

Amelia agreed and forced herself up from the kitchen table. "Okay. I'm so glad I have you right now, Yvette. You are the only thing holding me together." She leaned on her friend, and they walked back up the stairs arm in arm.

Sitting and waiting wasn't doing anything for either of their nerves. Yvette's mind was whirling trying to make sense of everything that had happened.

When the women arrived at the police station and requested to talk to Heath, they were directed to have a seat on the bench outside of his office while he finished up a meeting. Every time Yvette tried to focus on a possibility about who the victim could be or why no one had been able to get in touch with Mark, she was distracted by Amelia.

"How did his phone end up in the chicken coop of all places? It doesn't make any sense. Mark never went in there. He hired people to do that sort of thing." Amelia's left leg grazed Yvette's as they sat next to one another. She was wound tight. Her leg shook so hard she was causing the entire bench to vibrate with her movements.

"I don't know. I've seen him out on the farm before. Maybe he was just helping out."

Honestly, Yvette felt like she was grasping at straws. There really wasn't a reason she could think of why Mark's cell phone would have been found in the chicken coop, but it *was* a perfectly decent reason why he wasn't answering it. Not knowing the identity of the body that she'd seen wasn't a good sign, though. She scolded herself for not paying more attention even though deep down, she knew she'd reacted exactly how anyone else would have in such a situation. She grabbed a hold of Amelia's hand and gave it a light squeeze.

"I know you're only trying to make me feel better and I truly appreciate that, but I'm just nervous about Mark. You're the one who actually saw that awful mess, though. Do you want to talk about it?"

"Not really. I've been trying not to even think about it. It was a sight I never want to come across again and I don't mind not discussing it." Yvette stopped, hearing a shuffle of chairs coming from Heath's office.

The door across from them opened slowly and the

women looked up, both expecting to see Heath walking out to greet them.

"Mark! You're here. You're okay." Amelia raced over and threw her arms around him, nearly knocking him back.

Peering over Amelia's shoulder, Mark looked to Yvette with confusion on his face. "What are you two doing here?"

"We could ask you the same thing. We've been worried sick about you. Where have you been?" Yvette held up her hands in question.

"At home. I took a couple days off work so I could get some things taken care of. Heath stopped by and told me what happened at the lake house." He froze looking back and forth between the women. "The lake house... are you both okay? I'm so sorry you had to see that."

Amelia took a few slow steps backward to the bench and flopped down. "I'm so glad it wasn't you." She breathed a sigh of relief. "We have so much to talk about," she said, using a shaky hand to brush away a tear.

"You thought it was me? Why would I have been there? I knew you guys were going up there this weekend. It's not like I would have tried to crash your party or something."

Mark had gone to sit next to Amelia. He put his arm around her and tried to console her. Heath was still standing in the entrance of his office watching everything unfold in front of him. He turned to Yvette. "I have no idea what's happening right now. Is everything okay?"

"No. I mean yes. I don't know. We came here to tell you that we couldn't find Mark, and that someone from the farm found his phone. We were so worried it was him I saw out there."

Mark snapped his head up, overhearing Yvette. "They found my phone? I've been looking for that thing everywhere."

"Millie has it. That's why we're here. We thought something might have happened to you, but I'm glad you're okay," Yvette admitted.

Heath stepped into the hallway to join in on the conversation. "I'm glad you're all feeling a little relief, but the fact of the matter is, there was a body found and we don't have a lot of information right now. I'm going to need you three to stay alert and be certain to keep away from the lake house."

"Our stuff is still there. The only things they let us take were our purses. When can we get everything else?" Amelia asked Heath.

"I'll let you know." Heath's eyes scanned the

group. "Just make sure to be extra cautious and don't go getting any ideas on how to make sense of this." His eyes lingered on Yvette a little longer than the rest.

"We wouldn't dream of it," she replied, already plotting her next move.

CHAPTER SEVEN

Abigail brushed the hair from her daughter's eyes and handed her a steaming cup of tea.

"Don't beat yourself up, honey. You acted how anyone would have under the circumstances."

Yvette sniffled and rubbed the tears from her eyes. She gave her mom a half-smile. "I keep trying to tell myself that very same thing. I've been trying so hard to hold it together, but I think I need to give myself some time to process what happened."

"Oh, sweetie. You don't have to be strong all the time. It's okay to let it all out and feel something. What happened was a tragedy, and unfortunately, you were the one that had to witness it."

"I know, Mom. It's just hard not knowing anything yet. Heath hasn't released any information, no name, no arrest. I can't stop thinking about how whoever did this might be walking around town right next to me. I feel like I need to figure it out before someone else gets hurt or worse."

"The last thing you need to do is figure it out. We all want justice to be served but we need to leave that to the police. Why don't you finish up your tea and take a hot bath, then we can go out together and get something for lunch?"

Yvette sipped her tea, thankful she had someone to talk to. "I'll give it a shot," she said before rising to head upstairs.

Yvette felt much better as she pulled her shoes from the closet and slipped them on. Her mom had been right, the hot bath had soothed her nerves and now she was ready to take on the day. She went downstairs to tell her mom she was ready to leave and saw her dad coming up from the basement.

"Oh, shoot. I thought you were still upstairs," he told his daughter with a guilty look on his face.

"What's that?" Yvette asked, noticing the table he was lugging up the stairs.

"It was supposed to be a surprise." He sighed.

"For me? It's beautiful." Yvette peered around her dad, who was trying to hide an adorable little table in the shape of an ice cream cone. The bottom was made to look like an intricately designed sugar cone and the top was flat and looked like melted ice cream.

"I was working on them when you were here last week for dinner," Charlie confessed with a mischievous grin.

Yvette nudged her dad out of the way to get a better look. "Them? There's more than one?"

"I made enough for your whole shop. I'm taking this one to show everyone and tell them about the surprise. I was hoping I'd get it into the truck before you came downstairs."

"That's what the paint Heath brought over to the shop was for. I'm sorry I ruined your surprise, Dad, but I love these. They're going to look perfect in the shop." Yvette threw her arms around him. "Do you need any help with them or anything?"

"Not at all. I don't want you to lift a finger. I hope to have them all painted this week and set up for you soon after that. I may even enlist Joey for a little help."

"Joey? Really, Dad? Are you going soft on me?" Yvette giggled, knowing just how leery he was of her young employee and his troubled past.

"You say he's a good man, so I'll take your word for it."

"Are you ready to go?" Abigail interrupted, coming in from the kitchen. "Aww, you showed her the tables. You're so sweet. I know how you wanted them to be a surprise, but I think Yvette needed some happy news."

"Not exac..." Charlie began.

Yvette winked at her Dad. "Isn't he the best? I love them so much."

Charlie shook his head at his daughter. "Where are you girls off to?"

"Oh, I dunno. I think we'll stop somewhere for some food, then maybe we can go see Amelia." Yvette looked at her mother, hoping she wouldn't mind.

"I think that sounds like a great idea." Abigail agreed and gave her husband a quick peck on the cheek.

"See you later, Dad. Thanks again. I just love the tables." Yvette grinned before heading out the door for a day on the town with her mom. Sometimes being with her mother was all a girl needed to gain a little perspective and feel a whole heck of a lot better about things.

CHAPTER EIGHT

"Thanks for coming in. I feel bad I missed you and your mom when you came by the other day." Amelia waved Yvette into her office.

"It's okay, I know this time of year is busy for you." Yvette took a seat in the chair across from Amelia's.

With the holiday season getting ready to begin, Amelia would be working overtime until well after Christmas. The events that Heritage held were expansive and brought in hundreds of tourists each day. Amelia's career required her to be available nearly all day, every day from mid-September until after the new year. Yvette knew her friend had a lot on her plate, but she was hoping she'd be willing to talk with her for a few minutes.

"How are you?" Yvette asked, fidgeting with the strap on her purse.

"I'm feeling better, but I need to apologize to you. I was so worried about Mark that I didn't even consider your feelings. I know you were worried about him too and you were the one who found the body. I can't even believe I treated you the way I did. You're always the strong one who I lean on through all the hard times and it should have been the other way around this time. I'm sorry, truly sorry."

Yvette's eyes blurred with tears. "Thanks for that," she said genuinely. "I'm sorry too."

"Like I said, I'm really glad you stopped by. Have you heard anything from Heath?" Amelia asked.

"No, but I'm probably not the first on his list of people to call," Yvette's mouth twitched into a smile.

Amelia laughed. "I guess you're right. All I know is that they still haven't released any information about the identity of the man or how and why it happened. Oh, and my house is still a crime scene. Not that I want to go back there anytime soon or anything."

"I'm no professional, but I'd guess that he was stabbed by something. Repeatedly. There was so much blood." Yvette looked away and tried to wash the memory from her mind.

"I know it's hard, but we have to try to remember that the police are doing everything they can. In the meantime, we need to remember what Heath said. We've got to be cautious and stay aware of our surroundings."

"I agree." Yvette nodded. "We don't know who could have done this or why it happened at the house on the weekend we just happened to be going there."

Amelia sat up straighter in her seat. "What are you saying? You don't actually think it had anything to do with either of us, do you?"

"No, but that doesn't mean it hasn't crossed my mind. I told everyone I spoke to that I was going away and I'm sure you did the same, so it's entirely possible." Yvette shrugged.

"Great." Amelia huffed. "Another thing to worry about."

"Better safe than sorry. What did Mark say about everything?"

"He didn't really say anything. He thanked me for being so concerned and that was about it."

"What if we try to make him talk? Maybe he knows who the guy was."

"Don't you think Heath would have already asked him that?" Amelia asked.

"Yeah, probably. But I'd still like to know the

answer and I'm betting Heath won't be the one to tell me."

"I suppose not." Amelia chuckled. "I don't really want to see Mark right now though, is that okay? I'm still a little hurt I didn't get more of a reaction from him."

Yvette thought it was more than okay. Amelia might be her best friend, but she wasn't always held together very tightly, especially when it came to Mark. If she came along to talk to him, the conversation could sway to something else, and Yvette would never get anything accomplished.

"I get it. You don't have to come. I've been kind of slacking since this whole thing happened and haven't even stopped in at Sundae Afternoon. I could probably use a day to focus on work. I'll go to the farm and talk with Millie about some new ice cream flavors and then swing by Mark's office to see if I can get any information from him."

"What if he knows something? Do you think he'd hide it from me? Maybe that's why he's been so distant?" Amelia rattled off without taking a breath.

Yvette tried to reassure her friend. "I think you need to relax a little. I'm sure he isn't hiding anything from you. He probably didn't know the man. Maybe it was just a squatter who saw the place was empty more often than not."

"I don't know, but I want you to call me the minute you leave from talking with Mark!" Amelia demanded.

Yvette felt refreshed, ready to talk to Mark, and was thankful she'd finally gotten out of her funk. Seeing a body wasn't something she ever wanted to have happen again, but she knew she needed to move forward and get to the bottom of this. She had to make sure to keep it quiet, though, because the last thing she needed was her father and Heath on her tail.

CHAPTER NINE

Yvette spotted Millie through the window of her office and smiled. The conversation with the sweet, older woman was definitely going to be much easier than the one with Mark. On her way over, Yvette had called Sundae Afternoon to check in and see how inventory was looking and learned that her shop had been fairly busy all week and they were ready to place another order.

"Long time no see." Millie waved. "I'll be right there."

"Take your time." Yvette pulled out her phone to look over the list she'd made of flavors to try.

She'd been feeling a little less than creative lately, so she was excited to get some new flavors in the shop. She had a great idea while she was on her way to the farm. A banana frozen yogurt, with an extra-thick fudge ripple and little bits of homemade peanut butter fudge would be the perfect start to her first day back to work after her time off went horribly wrong.

"Sorry about that." Millie pulled the hairnet from atop her jet-black hair. "What can I do for ya?"

"No problem. I was hoping to place an order for a couple days from now."

Millie gestured for her to take a seat. "Sure thing. What'll be for this week?" she asked as she pulled out an order form.

"I think I'm going to switch everything up, actually. We still have enough of our regular stock to get us through the remainder of the week, but I'd like to end the summer with a bang and do some fruit flavors. Let's do blackberry and banana frozen yogurts, then for ice cream we'll do peach melba, blueberry lemonade, caramelized pear, some cherry vanilla, and the Malibu mango," she said, thinking fondly of her new neighbor.

"I don't think you've seen our latest order form yet, have you? We've added quite a few potential options for fall that I think you're going to love. I spent hours video chatting with Emma the other day, getting everything finalized." Millie handed over a few sheets of stapled paper.

"Not yet. I have to admit, though, no matter how ready I am for the seasons to change, I'm not quite sure everyone else is ready for it yet. I'd say we have a couple more weeks of our summer flavors before we switch over. Most people start craving pumpkin and maple and other flavors mid-September. The cozy feel of autumn tends to start a little later at our store since we stay open all year."

"What, you don't want to be like some of those stores that start setting up for Christmas in August?" Millie joked.

Yvette laughed and shook her head. "I love the holidays, and I'm always excited for them to roll around every year, but when all the other Sundae Afternoon's close, that means we get even busier. That's great for business but it also means super long days for all of us."

"No kidding. Who'd have thought that I'd be making ice cream in ten degree weather? Speaking of, I really need to get back to work. The Wildwood shop has a pretty hefty catering gig coming up and they tripled their normal order size."

"Whoa. Good for them. Thanks for carving out some time for me. I should have just called the order in." Yvette felt bad for interrupting Millie.

"Not at all. It's always good to see you, dear. You

may even be seeing my whole family soon. Got my grandkids coming to visit and I'm positive they'd love to stop by for an ice cream cone."

"I'll be looking forward to it."

Yvette thought about how much she'd enjoyed working with Millie over the years and having the chance to see her grandchildren grow. She thanked her and stood up to go find Mark, bracing herself for an interesting conversation.

CHAPTER TEN

"Mark! Hey, can I talk to you for a second?" Yvette yelled, hoping Mark had heard her. She saw him walking toward his truck and ran to catch up with him.

He turned around and looked surprised to see her headed his way. "What's going on?" he asked when she finally reached him.

"I've been thinking a lot about everything that happened at the lake house and I wanted to talk a little, that's all," she said once she caught her breath.

"Talk to me? Why? I mean, yeah, we can talk, I just don't understand why you'd choose me? We aren't exactly pals who do a lot of chitchatting." He raised a brow.

She needed to make sure she didn't do anything to

draw attention to herself that might make Mark realize she was trying to get information from him.

"It's just that my parents don't how I'm feeling, and I really don't want to bring my emotions to work or bother any of my employees. Plus, you're pretty even keeled in stressful situations, so I figured you'd be good to talk to."

"Well, if you're looking for even keeled, it makes sense why you didn't go to Amelia." Mark leaned against his truck with a slight grin on his face.

"Hey, someone was killed in her house. Give her a break," Yvette scolded.

"It's my house too," Mark reminded her.

"I know. You're right and I'm sorry. Have you heard anything more about it?"

"Yvette. We shouldn't be talking about this."

Now we're getting somewhere, she thought. *If he knows something, Heath would have definitely told him not to discuss it with anyone.*

Yvette tried to play it cool and leaned back on the truck next to Mark. "What do you mean? Do you know something? Did they release the man's identity or something?"

"If they did, you'd have heard it on the news, no?"

She gave him her best puppy dog eyes. "I'm

nervous, Mark. This is the second time I've been around a murder. I always thought Heritage was a safe place to live."

"I know it's hard to believe right now, but it is a safe place. This is your home, and the fact that this is the second time you've been around a murder is exactly why we shouldn't be having this conversation." Mark gave her a stern look.

"There's nothing you can say to ease my mind a little? Please?" she begged.

"You're worse than my sister." Mark shook his head, but Yvette knew she was getting to him.

"Pretty please? I know you know something."

"Fine, but you need to keep this to yourself. I promised Heath I wouldn't share anything."

Yvette breathed a sigh of relief. "Okay, I promise," she said, crossing her fingers behind her back just in case that sort of thing made a difference.

Mark's eyes darted around before he said anything. "I rented out the house to a couple that came by the farm. I overheard the man on the phone saying they were looking for a place to stay while they were in town, and I thought about the lake house. No one had been using it, so I didn't think it would cause any harm. They said they were only going to be there for a few days, and they'd be gone before you and Amelia planned on getting to the house."

Yvette mind swirled with questions. "You knew him? Was it the same guy? Where was his wife? Wait, was she the one that killed him?"

"Don't do that. Don't get yourself all riled up." Mark pinched the bridge of his nose.

Yvette saw he was frustrated so she tried to dial it down a notch. She needed more information but had to go about it differently otherwise Mark would stop talking.

"Okay, so what do you know then? Is the guy I found the one you rented the house to?" she asked.

"I don't know. I didn't even really get a good look at him, honestly. He spent the majority of the time on the phone while the woman and I set up the rental. She claimed she wanted to surprise him. I told Heath about them, but I didn't have anything aside from the woman's name. She paid in cash. I gave her a receipt but then I found it on the ground by where their car was parked. I didn't think much of it at the time and don't even know if it matters now."

"How could you have been so careless? You didn't even get both of their names and you let them in your house?"

"It's not like we keep any valuables there or

anything. No one had even been at the house in months. The woman seemed normal enough and they were just passing through, so I figured, why not do something nice to help them out? You've been telling me I should be nicer to people, haven't you?"

"I can appreciate that, but it didn't really turn out how you expected, did it?"

"I guess not, but it's not like I should have expected something like this to happen, either." Mark threw his hands in the air. "All I know is that the woman's name is Marissa Ashford, they both looked to be in their late twenties, and they were visiting from Vermont."

"Wow. Well, obviously you haven't told Amelia anything about this yet."

"Definitely not. She'd have my head if she knew I rented out the house and didn't tell her. I'd really love it if you didn't tell her either." Mark's eyes narrowed.

Yvette couldn't believe what she was hearing. It was possible the couple had nothing to do with the man she'd found, but it didn't make what Mark had done any better. Being kind was one thing but being careless was another.

"I won't tell her, but you can't keep it from her for too long. Everything will come out sooner or later and you'll regret not having told her yourself if she finds out some other way."

Mark promised to tell Amelia the truth and reminded Yvette not to get involved any further.

On the walk back to her SUV, Yvette planned the rest of her day and made sure to include having time with her laptop to search for social media accounts belonging to Marissa Ashford. Surely a woman in her twenties would be easy to find online.

CHAPTER ELEVEN

"I think I'm going to plan a staff meeting for right before I leave to go to Townsend," Yvette said to her part-time employee, Tonya, as she flipped the shop's sign to CLOSED.

Tonya nodded. "I still can't believe you're going over there. It's about time Henry gets his act together, though. I don't mean to be rude but how many times have we covered for him now?"

"Hopefully I can get a few ideas as to why things seem so messy over there lately. We need to find a way for him to get organized before the whole place falls apart. One thing I do know is that at least one of his staff members is awesome. I was so proud of Max when he was here. Maybe he'll consider coming over here for a few shifts once the Townsend location closes for the winter. I think we'd be lucky to have him."

Yvette knew how frustrated her staff was with Henry but was able to see the bigger picture. She knew how important it was for Sundae Afternoon as a whole to help him out no matter how they felt about him personally. A staff meeting would ensure that everyone at her shop knew what was going on and was prepared to be without her for a week. She always wanted them to know how proud she was of each of them and all of their hard work.

"Ohmigosh, have you two tried the banana yogurt yet? It's out of this world," Vanessa gushed as she came from the kitchen.

"I'm not big on frozen yogurt." Tonya pulled her apron off of her tiny frame.

"You have to at least try it. You don't know what you're missing." Vanessa pulled two sample spoons from the mason jar on the counter.

"I have a much better idea. Why don't you let me go in the back and whip up something really quickly? Give me about ten minutes and I'll meet you back out here." Yvette gestured for her employees to take a seat in the dining area.

Running an ice cream shop had its perks. Yvette

ordered all of the ice cream from the farm, but she loved being able to use it to create something new. She took the banana frozen yogurt from the freezer and spotted something she thought would be a perfect addition to the final product. She sprinkled a bed of milk chocolate shavings on the bottom of an oblong glass dish and placed three scoops of yogurt on top, one for each of them. She sliced the peanut butter fudge as thinly as she could and layered the slices between each scoop and then added some on top for good measure. Finally, she took her secret ingredient and drizzled it over the top of the sundae. Yvette didn't want to take away from the flavors she'd mixed, so she decided to skip the whipped cream this time. She carefully lifted the dish from the counter, afraid to wreck her creation, and made her way back out front.

"Put away those silly sample spoons, girls. I've got a treat for you!" Yvette grinned when she saw the looks on her employees' faces.

"What is that delicious looking thing?" Vanessa eyed the sundae as Yvette set it down on the table in front of her.

"Well, when I ordered the banana yogurt, I was going to have Millie add a fudge ripple to it, but I changed my mind at the last minute and decided to create this instead. Dig in, I can't wait to hear what you think!"

"Spoons. We need spoons!" Tonya exclaimed, jumping up to retrieve some from behind the counter.

"Here, you take the first bite," Vanessa said, handing Yvette a spoon. "You're the mastermind behind it all."

Yvette filled the spoon high with a little bit of everything from the dish. "It's pretty delicious if I do say so myself."

"Is that honey I'm tasting?" Tonya asked as she swallowed a mouthful.

"I don't even care what it is," Vanessa said, wiping her chin with a napkin. "This is so good. I'm glad you didn't order the fudge ripple because this is about as close to perfection as you can get."

Yvette took another spoonful before telling them the ingredients and letting them know it would be on special for the rest of the week.

"So, I think we need to have a staff meeting before I leave. Do either of you have a suggestion on when we should have it?" Yvette looked to her employees.

"Doesn't matter to me. And as long as we're doing it before you leave, I don't think it will matter to Sage either," Vanessa answered for herself and her daughter.

"I had plans, but it seems they're canceled now." Tonya took the last bite of her share of the sundae. "Some friends were supposed to be in town, but they never showed up."

"Well, I like to be as accommodating as possible, so let me know if you hear anything in the next few days and then we can set a date," Yvette said.

"I think I'll give them another call right now, actually. I have a few things left to do around here to close up but if you don't mind me using my phone, I can do it at the same time." Tonya looked to her boss for approval.

"I'll help you do some of your work, so we can both get out of here faster," Vanessa offered.

"Sure, go ahead and give them a call and just let me know." Yvette rose from the table and took the dish and spoons with her. "Whatever works for you guys, works for me."

She dropped off the dishes in the kitchen and was heading to her office to count the register and run a sales report when she remembered she'd left the work phone sitting on the table.

"I don't know why you even have a phone if you

aren't going to bother answering it, Marissa. Call me back, I need to know if you're still coming or not."

It sounded like Tonya was leaving a voicemail and Yvette stopped dead in her tracks when she'd heard the name Marissa. She didn't want to worry Tonya or involve her in something so tragic for no reason, but when Yvette wasn't able to find any information online about Marissa Ashford, she wasn't sure what her next step would be.

Now, she may have walked right into a clue about who was in the lake house that day. She needed to decide the best way to ask Tonya a few questions without being too obvious.

CHAPTER TWELVE

Yvette was not only avoiding her best friend, but also her parents. She felt terrible, but she knew it was better if they didn't know she was digging around. Today was her day off from work and she'd hoped to sit down and construct a plan on how to confront Tonya about what she'd heard the day before. With a coffee in one hand and a homemade breakfast burrito in the other, Yvette lounged on her cream-colored porch swing, planning to enjoy a few moments to herself.

"Yes, I understand Mr. Gardner. Uh huh, yes. I'm sorry. I'll be there as soon as I can to take care of that for you." Gavin spoke into his cell phone as he came out his front door.

"What was that all about?" Yvette sat up and turned her head in his direction.

"Oh, that was Mr. Gardner. He needs me to come over right away because he has squirrels trying to get into his bird feeders. He's in a panic because they're taking away the food from his birds."

"What are you supposed to do about that?" She laughed. "You know, I think I saw something online once about how you can put oil or petroleum jelly along the poles where the feeders are, so the squirrels slide down or something."

"Well, that's a great idea except the problem is that he has a remote-control truck he uses to startle the squirrels, so they run away, but he crashed it," Gavin explained. "He ran it right into his well pump and it broke a piece off, so there's water squirting out all over the place and he can't figure out how to turn off the water."

Yvette raised her brows. "Oh. That's way out of my expertise. Mr. Gardner sure is an interesting man."

"He's certainly something. I'll be back," Gavin said.

Yvette was glad that she only had a few people to worry about. Granted she had customers in and out of the shop all day and employees to tend to, but Gavin owned several apartment buildings and homes and was responsible for everything, every single time something went wrong. And as Mr. Gardner had proven, some of his tenants were more difficult than others.

She forced herself out of the daze she was in, and knew she had to come up with a plan. She was going to have to ask Tonya about her phone call. She promised Mark she wouldn't tell Amelia what was going on, but she might have to tell Tonya. Her quiet time had already been interrupted, so she decided to go inside and get ready for the day.

She threw on some shorts and a t-shirt, slid her feet into her favorite pair of sandals and grabbed her purse before heading out the door. Yvette drove to Sundae Afternoon hoping to chat with Tonya before the shop got too busy.

———

"Oh, hey, boss." Tonya smiled when she saw Yvette walk through the dining area. "What are you doing here?"

"I was wondering if you had a few minutes to chat." Yvette looked and saw a single customer in a corner booth and motioned for Tonya to follow her to the other side of the store.

Tonya raised a brow. "Sure, is something wrong?"

"I don't know." Yvette sighed. "I'm assuming you heard about the body they found at the lake house?"

"The body *you* found, you mean? No one wanted to bring it up, but we all know what happened."

Yvette rubbed her hands together and continued, "They still haven't released the identity of the man and there's something I overheard you saying on the phone that I was hoping you'd be able to clear up."

"Me? Of course. How can I help?" Tonya's eyes flashed with worry.

"You mentioned you were having friends come to town. Did they ever show up?"

"Umm, no. What is this about?" Tonya asked.

Yvette dove into the story Mark had told her and was hoping those people weren't Tonya's friends. "So, when I heard you say the name Marissa on the phone the other day, my mind immediately went back to what Mark had said."

The color drained from Tonya's face. "That's Marissa." She pointed to the lone woman in the shop. "She and her fiancé, Jordan, got into a fight and she hasn't seen him since it happened. They're here visiting Marissa's cousins, but Jordan didn't want to stay with them the entire time because they'd never really gotten along with one another, and they had some other family coming to town as well. So, instead of being uncomfortable and cramped in the house, they were looking for a cheap place to stay for a few nights. You don't think…"

"Do you think she'd mind if I asked her a few questions?"

"Let me ask her. Should I tell her what's going on?

"No, let me talk to her first. I don't want to cause her any concern if I'm wrong."

Yvette took a deep breath and held her head high as she walked over to the table to greet Marissa.

———

After Yvette explained everything to her, and after several minutes of heavy tears, Marissa finally began to calm down.

"So, I guess I'll go to the police, but I don't even know what to say." Marissa sniffled.

"Ask for Heath. Tell him who you are and everything you know about Jordan. Any information you have will be helpful," Yvette reassured the woman.

"He has no real family around. No one but me, anyway. Poor Jordan. I've been so mad at him for taking off and he might… oh gosh, he might be dead." Marissa broke down again.

"That's why it's so important for you to go to the police. I understand how worried you are, but the sooner you can help answer any questions, the sooner all of this can get figured out."

"I understand. I'll do everything I can."

"Do you mind if I ask why he left? Did you two have a fight?" Yvette hoped she didn't give herself away. She didn't want the woman to know that Tonya had already shared that with her.

Marissa fiddled with the napkin dispenser on the table. "I should have known something like this would happen. Every time Jordan gets upset, he over-reacts, and we get into a fight. I was so sick of arguing that I did something I thought would be help-ful, but like Jordan always says, my crazy ideas never amount to anything good."

Yvette tensed, opening up her mouth to speak.

"Don't get me wrong," Marissa continued, noticing Yvette's surprised reaction, "Jordan is a good man. He was already upset because I didn't tell him I was planning on having us stay at my cousin's house while we were in the area. Those two never really got along, especially recently. We were hoping to have a quiet wedding on the fifteenth of next month but that was the same date they picked. They'd been planning a larger wedding, so we agreed to push ours out a bit since we only had a small guest list. He knows how much this wedding means to me and was angry because thought I'd caved like I always do."

"So, that's how you two ended up staying at the lake house?"

Marissa nodded. "We were on our way out of Merryville from my cousin's house. We'd just spoken to my aunt Darla, and she was giving us a hard time about wedding stuff. She'd been trying to make sure our decorations and food choices weren't too similar to my cousin's, and things had quickly gotten out of hand. We left and went for a drive which is when we saw the farm. We decided to stop there to walk around a little and try to calm down. My aunt called Jordan to keep yelling at him and when he was busy talking, I met the guy you told me about. He offered to let us stay a few nights out at the lake and I took him up on the offer right away. I wanted to surprise Jordan and try to end the fight we were having about the wedding so I paid as quickly as I could. I wanted to salvage what was left of our trip, not cause problems. Her eyes welled with tears.

Yvette reached across the table and offered the

woman her hand. "Can I get you some water or anything?"

"No, thanks." She wiped away her tears. "Thank you for being so nice. I haven't been able to get in touch with Jordan, and he didn't take our car, so I thought maybe he just took a cab home or something. I came to apologize to Tonya for basically blowing her off. She knows how Jordan is though, and never did agree with me sticking by his side since he was always such a short fuse. But he was only like that when it came to making sure I was happy. He loved me."

"Tonya has always been a great judge of character, and it's good to have friends around that have your best interest at heart," Yvette said honestly.

"She's a great friend, for sure. I'm so glad I was able to talk to you or I'd have left and never known a thing."

"I'm happy to help. Anyone who is a friend of Tonya's is a friend of mine. Speaking of, I'll send her right over." Yvette rose from the table and put a hand on Marissa's shoulder before heading to her office.

She didn't believe Tonya had anything to do with Jordan's death, no matter how much she didn't like someone. She wasn't going to even entertain the thought. Yvette wanted a distraction from what she'd just learned, so she turned on her computer and began working on payroll for the week. She was interrupted by her phone dinging, signaling a text message. She pulled it from her back pocket and saw a frantic text from Amelia.

Where have you been?!

I just talked to Mark! You aren't gonna believe this!

I'm working from home today, come over NOW!!

Yvette needed to talk to someone, and now that Mark had finally told Amelia that he knew more than he'd originally let on, she could confide in her and hopefully figure out a little more about Jordan and who could have killed him. So far, the only person who even knew him was the sweet woman Yvette had just met. Certainly, she couldn't have had anything to do with it. Amelia was always good at working things out that seemed difficult to understand, so hopefully this was a puzzle she was willing to help solve.

CHAPTER THIRTEEN

Having been friends for several years, Yvette knew exactly what the look on Amelia's face meant when she saw her.

"You already knew?" Amelia asked, hands on her hips.

She let out a breath and stared at her feet. "I'm sorry," she admitted. "I didn't want you getting upset with Mark. I'm sure he thought they were just a sweet young couple in need. It's not like he could have known what would happen. For all we know, they might actually be a sweet young couple who have nothing to do with any of this. I met Marissa earlier, and she was lovely."

"You met them! You knew about this for that long without telling me?"

Yvette saw the hurt in her friend's eyes. "If you'd just hear me out, I think we can make some sense of this. Please?"

"Fine." She sighed, shaking her head.

"After I went to talk to Mark and learned he'd rented out the house but didn't get any information from the people other than a single name, I went searching online but couldn't find anything. I can't even begin to tell you all the ideas that were running through my mind, but I didn't know which direction to go. I thought I'd reached a dead-end until I over-heard Tonya on the phone, using the same name that Mark had told me. Once I decided to talk to her about it, I stumbled across even more information and that's what I'm hoping we can discuss." Yvette sat back in the chair; hopeful her friend would agree.

"I'm still mad you didn't tell me, and I hate that you are so caught up in this but go ahead…"

"Once I finally got the courage to talk to Tonya, I ended up actually meeting Marissa," Yvette explained the conversation she'd had with the woman.

Amelia's jaw dropped. "You said she was lovely, but it seems to me that she's the only person who could have killed him."

"What makes you say that?"

"She said they were fighting and that he overreacted often. What if that's the case here too? Maybe the fight got so bad that she couldn't handle the arguing, so she killed him to make it stop and now she's just pretending to be the nice person you think she is?"

"I'd normally say that's ridiculous, but Marissa did tell me that Jordan wasn't very kind when it came to her ideas of how to fix their relationship. I suppose it's possible she could have done it."

"Of course, it's possible, Yvette! You don't know anything about these people."

"That's exactly why I'm going to learn more about them. We need to know more about Marissa's family. It's not fair to blame only Marissa when we don't know the whole story."

"You're going to get me in trouble one day." Amelia shifted in her seat, but her face gave her away as a willing participant.

"I knew I could count on you." Yvette grinned. "Okay, so, Heath hasn't released the name of the victim yet, but I told Marissa she needed to go talk to him and tell him everything she knew. If it was her fiancé I found, she needs some closure."

"There's something missing, though. Mark rented our house to these people, only knowing the woman's name and then when you talked to her, she said that

Jordan had no family, just her. Is he some mystery guy or something with no family, no friends, and no name? Isn't it odd both of them didn't talk to Mark? I know you said she was trying to surprise him, but it still seems strange. Maybe the guy was into some bad stuff. We can't just assume they're good people."

Yvette didn't know what to think, but she really wanted to get to the bottom of things. She felt ten times better being able to talk to Amelia about it and as long as she could stay off of Heath's radar for a while, there was still time for her to figure things out.

"Seems like Marissa is the mysterious one." Yvette shrugged as she scrolled on her phone. "I can't find a single thing about her online. I even looked up the lake to see if she tagged any photos of herself there or something."

"All this information is frying my brain. Want to go get something to eat or go shopping or something while we talk more?" Amelia asked, grabbing her purse.

"Sounds good. We can do both, but let's start with food. That always makes me feel better."

"This is fantastic," Yvette said between bites of her turkey and cranberry wrap.

Amelia agreed and picked up a sweet potato fry from her own plate. "The bistro always has the best lunch specials. I come here all the time when I'm working."

"I'm sorry I interrupted your day. You said you were working from home, and I just barged right in."

"That's not quite how it happened." Amelia chuckled. "I told you to come over, and I was having a hard time getting inspired at home, anyway. I'm working from home all week and have a huge tour coming up for Halloween, but I can't seem to settle on anything."

Yvette's eyes narrowed. "It's August."

"I know, I know. It's still far away, but you know how the holiday season works around here. I won't have a day off for weeks once October gets here so I like to start early."

"I can help you do some planning if you want. It may do me some good to get my mind off murder for a few minutes," Yvette offered.

The women were deep in conversation, working on ideas for the Heritage Halloween Tour when a voice they both recognized interrupted them.

"Hey, ladies, how ya doing?" Heath Briggs asked, standing at the end of their table.

"What are you doing here?" Yvette blurted out.

"Jeez, Yvette. I'm getting a grilled cheese for lunch." Heath looked surprised.

"I'm sorry, I didn't mean it like that. I'm surprised to see you is all. I know I shouldn't be asking but I was wondering if Marissa's information was any help in your investigation?"

"Marissa? How do you know about Marissa?" Heath stepped back, confusion in his eyes.

"Oh, good, so she did stop by. I feel so bad for that poor woman. I can't imagine what she's going through." Amelia lowered her head.

"I'm not exactly sure what you two are talking about. I haven't spoken to Marissa and I'm not even sure how you know about her," he said before taking a seat.

"I just met her this morning. She's friends with Tonya from work. I told her she needed to meet with you and fill you in on a few things. She thought her fiancé was mad and left town but now I'm thinking that he may have been the one at the lake house."

"I've been at the station all morning until about fifteen minutes ago. I'm not really following what you're saying. Are you positive she was coming?" Heath asked.

"I am. She was a nervous wreck."

"Listen, girls, I need you to stay clear of this whole mess." Heath sighed. "I suppose there's no harm in telling you since we'll be releasing the information later today. The body was identified as Jordan Ashford and his next of kin has been notified. We've been looking for Marissa since I spoke with Mark. I'm assuming he's the one who told you about her." Heath rubbed his chin. "We haven't been able to make contact with her and she's our lead suspect. Now, where did you say you saw her?" he asked.

Yvette's expression dulled. "At Sundae Afternoon, earlier today. She was there to see Tonya and when I realized who she was, I talked with her for a few minutes. It seemed like she was genuinely concerned when I told her what was going on. I urged her to meet with you and she assured me she would."

Heath grimaced and leaned forward in his chair. "You need to stay out of this and stay away from her. She may be dangerous. I'm the one that should be talking to her, not you." He gave Yvette a stern look.

"She didn't know," Amelia defended her. "Mark was the one who rented the house to strangers."

"I've got to go. Maybe I can still catch her at your

shop." Heath went out the front door of the bistro without even ordering his lunch.

Yvette was shocked. This was the second time she had come face to face with someone who might be a killer and didn't know it. She was quickly learning that her judge of character wasn't as good as she thought. Maybe Heath was right, it was time for her to stay out of this.

"I think I lost my appetite," Amelia said, pushing her plate away.

"Me too. I'll drop you off, and then I'm going home myself to relax and unwind a little. This has been a crazy day."

CHAPTER FOURTEEN

Gavin came trudging up the porch steps, covered in mud.

"What happened to you?" Yvette cackled when she saw him.

"Mr. Gardner happened."

Yvette burst out laughing again. "I thought you only had to go shut off his water, and that was hours ago."

"So did I. Instead of just letting the water spray out though, he decided it would be better to catch it in buckets and use it to water his plants. I'm all for saving water, but he asked if I'd help carry the buckets into the house for him. Being the nice guy that I am, I agreed. But then his little dog got out and started chasing a squirrel, and I had my hands full. I tried to dodge the dog, but I tripped over him, dropped all the water, and landed in the mud. And now… I don't like squirrels any more than Mr. Gardner does." Gavin glanced down at himself. "I need a shower."

Yvette could always count on Gavin to entertain her. "Yes, you really do."

Her mind was reeling, and she wanted to stay in the comfort of her own home and not worry about anything else for the rest of the day. She thought Gavin's idea of a shower was a good one, so she gathered her things from the table and went inside to take one of her own.

Yvette had only been out of the shower for a few minutes when she heard a noise downstairs. She wasn't expecting any company and was certain she'd locked her doors. She grabbed her phone and slowly made her way down the stairs.

"This is ridiculous. I need to stop being so jumpy," she said aloud when she realized she'd left the living room window open and what she'd heard was the postman delivering a package to Gavin.

Just then, the phone rang in her hand, and she nearly dropped it. She turned it over to look at the caller ID. It was Tonya.

"Hello?" Yvette paced, hoping that whatever Tonya had to say was good news.

"Are you sure?" Yvette asked after listening to her employee for a moment. "But I told Heath that Marissa was going to stop by, and he told me she never showed up." Yvette froze as a thought occurred to her. "I have to go." She hung up and immediately dialed Heath at the police station.

"I'm sorry, but when they said you weren't back from lunch yet, I knew I had to come find you," Yvette said, trying to catch her breath from running from her car into Carlisle's Bistro. "I know you didn't get to order earlier so I just assumed I'd find you here."

"It's fine. I'm just trying to enjoy my lunch, Yvette. What can I do for you?"

"We've been looking for Marissa Ashford, but that's not her name. That's Jordan's last name but they aren't married yet. When you told me the body had been identified as Jordan Ashford, I remembered that she'd told me they'd put off their wedding because it was going to be the same date as one of their family members. Her last name wouldn't be Ashford yet. I talked to Tonya, and she said Marissa was gone. She tried calling her several times, but she wasn't answering. She also told me Marissa's last name was Raven. We need to be looking for Marissa Raven not Marissa Ashford."

"Whoa." He held up his hands. "First of all, you need to take a breath and calm down for a second. Second, it's me who needs to be looking for Marissa Raven. You need to be doing nothing of the sort."

"But…"

"No." Heath's voice was stern. "You really need to stay out of this. The woman may have killed her fiancé, and she basically gave a fake name to Mark. I appreciate your dedication to this, but you need to let me do my job." Heath stood and offered to walk Yvette to the door.

Frustrated, she agreed.

"Go home and enjoy the rest of your day off," he told her.

Yvette decided to stop in at Sundae Afternoon to see if Tonya had heard anything else. Going home to enjoy what was left of her day wasn't going to happen. Even if Tonya didn't have any more information, something about being at Sundae Afternoon with the buzz of happy customers always made her feel a little better about things. One way or another, she was going to do what she could to settle her nerves, whether it be solving a murder or drowning herself in cookie dough ice cream.

CHAPTER FIFTEEN

Yvette stepped into the shop and couldn't believe how busy they were. Tonya and Vanessa were running around from table to table, taking orders and making sure the guests were happy. Joey was dashing back and forth from the dining area to the kitchen, his hands full of dishes. Sage and Sundae Afternoon's newest employee, Stella, were trading between scooping ice cream and running the register. She saw at least four families waiting by the door for a place to sit and even the outdoor tables were full. She tossed her things in her office and hopped behind the counter to help dish out a few sundaes.

"Yvette, hey! Can you make me a kid's banana split, hold the cherries? The little boy it belonged to dropped it," Vanessa asked as she breezed past the counter.

She sliced a banana, dropped a half scoop each of vanilla, chocolate, and strawberry ice creams, added a drizzle of hot fudge and marshmallow, put a few strawberries on top and a dollop of whipped cream and passed it to Vanessa as she dashed by again. She was heading to help clean up the mess when she saw Joey already on his hands and knees taking care of it. Yvette saw each member of her staff effectively doing their jobs and decided to make a loop around the dining area to greet her customers.

Barry Bradford and his wife, Kelly, were at one of the tables outside and she headed in their direction first. Out of the corner of her eye, she noticed her neighbor, Jamie, and her fiancé, Evan, sitting on a bench by the door waiting for a table.

"Hi, you two! I'm so glad you came in. I made sure to order some Malibu Mango for you." Yvette winked at Jamie.

"You're here! We've been sitting for about ten minutes or so and were looking around for you. We were hoping to talk to you about something, but it looks like it's a little too busy in here today for that."

Yvette glanced around the shop. "That's for sure. I planned on being here for just a few minutes but when I saw how busy it was, I jumped in to help. It looks like everything under control right now, though. How about once you get seated, I'll stop over, and we can talk?"

"That'd be great. We were hoping you could do us a small favor, is all." Evan tucked his hands into his pockets.

"Of course." Yvette smiled warmly at the young couple. "I'll do whatever I can."

"Hello, Miss. Are you the owner?" a small voice came from behind her.

Turning around, she saw the boy who had dropped his sundae. "I'm the manager," she said, kneeling down to the boy's level. "My name's Yvette. What can I do for you?"

"I'm Jerry Pursley and I'm eight years old. I wanted to say that I was sorry for making a mess." He stuck out his hand and proudly offered her a small coin and a business card.

"What's this?" Yvette asked.

"It's a token for my lemonade stand and a business card that has my address on it. I open my stand every weekend in the front yard. I wanted to give you one, so you can come over and get a free cup. I pass them out to people sometimes and I thought that since I made such a mess at your place, you might like one." He pulled another token out of his pocket. "If you could, give one to the nice man who helped clean up."

Yvette looked into the blond-haired boy's eyes. "That's very generous of you, Jerry. You are quite the business man. I will absolutely give this to Joey and tell him what you said. I'll make sure we both stop and see you and your lemonade stand and we'll even bring along some friends."

"I'd like that. Thank you." Jerry smiled brightly and hurried back to the table to where his parents sat, beaming proudly.

Yvette's heart swelled at the young boy's kindness. She'd said coming into Sundae Afternoon would calm and rejuvenate her, but she'd not expected something like this. In her mind, the good in the world outweighed the bad every time and she refused to get sucked up in any negativity. Meeting Jerry was exactly what she'd needed to brighten her spirits.

Yvette got back to work. She glanced out the window and saw that Barry and Kelly were gone from the table and Evan and Jamie sat in their place. She looked around the shop and saw things had calmed down a little more. Now was as good of a time as any for her to go and see what they'd needed from her.

"Have you ordered yet?" Yvette asked once she'd reached their table.

"Yup. Our friend Tonya took our order. I didn't know she worked here," Jamie answered.

"You guys know Tonya? That's great. She's been here a little less than a year and we love having her around."

Evan shifted in his seat. "She's friends with my cousin. They used to work together back in the day."

"Small world," Yvette said. "That's the thing about small towns though, everyone ends up knowing everyone."

"Anyway, we know it might be a little inconvenient, but as you know we're getting married soon and the restaurant that was supposed to cater for us isn't able to anymore. We were hoping you might have some time and wouldn't mind doing it for us?" Jamie said softly.

"Well," Yvette said, gesturing around the shop. "As you can see we don't serve anything besides ice cream here so I'm afraid we wouldn't be able to offer you exactly what you're looking for."

The couple looked at one another and exchanged a grin. Evan spoke first. "We know, but that's okay. We had actually discussed doing an ice cream social at one point, until my mom basically threw a hissy fit when she heard our idea. She's very particular about our wedding."

"We'd love you to do it if you are able." Jamie looked hopeful.

"What's the date of your wedding? I can check our schedule and see if we have any conflicts but aside from that I don't see why it wouldn't be possible."

"September fifteenth," they said in unison.

Yvette tried to hide any hint of realization on her face when she'd heard the date of their wedding. That was the same date that Marissa had used, and Evan just said that Tonya was friends with his cousin.

"I'll look over my calendar as soon as I get to my office."

Yvette had never been more grateful that she'd slid her phone into her pocket before coming over to the table. Pulling it out as discreetly as she could, she used speed dial to call the shop's number.

"Oops, I better get that!" Yvette exclaimed. "I'll check on your order while I'm up."

Yvette got up from the table as quickly as she could and dashed to her office, grabbing the landline on her way by.

CHAPTER SIXTEEN

Yvette pounded on Gavin's door as hard as she could with one hand and texted Amelia with the other. She'd all but run home after she left the shop and was ready to burst.

"What's wrong?" Gavin asked after he'd opened the door.

Yvette pushed the door open further and blew past him into his kitchen. "Tell me everything you know about Evan and Jamie," she demanded.

"I don't know any more than you, I don't think, why?"

Yvette rattled off the story about Marissa and Jordan and what Evan and Jamie had just asked her. Gavin was shaking his head the entire time. "What? Why are you doing that?" she snapped at him.

"You're still interfering in this? Have you told Heath?"

"I don't need to hear that right now. I need your help. Amelia is on her way over and I need you two to help me figure this out." Yvette put her hands on her hips.

"How much more do you need to know? Mark rented the place out to a couple of weirdos, the girl killed her jerk boyfriend and took off, end of story. Seems pretty cut and dry to me."

"I see what you're saying, but it just doesn't feel right."

Gavin rolled his eyes. "You think Heath uses his feelings to solve crimes?"

"Of course not." Her face was getting redder by the minute. "There are several suspects now and every one of them could be responsible for killing Jordan."

Amelia knocked on the door a single time and let herself in. "Hey, Gavin, good to see you." She raised her hand in half a wave before sitting down next to Yvette at the table.

"I swear, the two of you are something else. Just call Heath. I'm staying out of it." Gavin walked out to the porch.

"Before you say anything, I have something to tell you." Amelia's eyes were wild.

"But this is important!" Yvette replied.

"I met Marissa," Amelia blurted out.

"What? She's still here? Where?"

"She came to my office with another woman. I assumed it was her mom. She said she wanted to talk to me and apologize for renting the house. She felt like she needed to get it off her chest before she went to the police."

Yvette tilted her head. "How did she know where you worked or that it was your house?"

Amelia frowned. "I didn't ask. I just figured you told her when you talked to her."

"I guess I might have. I was so flustered; I really don't know what I said."

Amelia continued, "It's okay. I thought she was nice. She was so upset about losing her fiancé and didn't understand what could have happened. They'd been arguing about their wedding and how annoyed he was with her for agreeing to put it on hold. She felt like she did the right thing since they were only going to have a small gathering. She told me that she got really angry when Jordan told her that he'd called the caterer for her cousin's wedding and canceled, pretending to be the groom. She told him she didn't want to marry a guy who could do something so awful and then she took off."

Yvette's eyes were wide, and her body was tense. "Canceled the caterer?"

"Umm, yeah. That's what she said. What does that have to do with anything?"

"The reason I called you here was because I just left Jamie and Evan, my new neighbors. I'm pretty sure Evan is Marissa's cousin. They stopped in at Sundae Afternoon to ask if I'd cater their wedding because their caterer was no longer available."

"Do you think one of them could have done it? Amelia asked.

"I don't know, but I think Gavin was right. We need to go see Heath at the police station. These people could be dangerous."

"I'm going to need you girls to go somewhere safe. Stay together and make sure you don't get involved any more than you already are," Heath told the women once Yvette had relayed everything she knew.

"I know you're mad, but we were only trying to help." Amelia tugged on the collar of her shirt.

"I'm not mad, I'm worried. Neither of you should be this deep in the case. I know it was your house Amelia, and you were both there but that doesn't mean the next logical step is to solve the crime. Now, go and please keep to yourselves. I'll be looking into the information you gave me."

Yvette and Amelia left his office, both feeling like they'd helped at least a little. They did their part, and now, it was up to Heath to do the rest.

"I don't see how there are so many people who could have potentially killed someone in our little town. Marissa could have killed her fiancé because of his bad temper. Jamie and Evan could be responsible because they were forced to adjust their wedding plans, and I know that would make me angry… maybe not enough to kill someone, but still. And then there's Tonya. She's spunky and never tolerates anything. If she didn't like the way her friend was being treated, then it's certainly possible she did something about it." Amelia rambled as the two headed back to the SUV.

"Don't start. There is no way Tonya did this. Last time everyone thought it was Joey. I refuse to get it stuck in my head that all my employees are potential killers."

"I'm just saying. It's definitely not a cut and dry

situation." Amelia sunk into the passenger seat and sat in silence as they made their way back to Yvette's house.

CHAPTER SEVENTEEN

Yvette made sure her doors were locked, and the curtains were drawn. She carried two plates of cookies from the kitchen while Amelia followed behind with two glasses of milk. They'd listened to Heath and gone back to Yvette's house for the remainder of the day. The women sat, picking listlessly at their snickerdoodles and milk while streaming romantic comedies to try and take their minds off things.

"Do you hear that?" Amelia asked, nearly jumping out of her chair.

Yvette strained to listen. "We're just anxious, everything's fine."

"No. I hear sirens. Shhh, listen." Amelia put her finger to her lips.

Yvette got up from the couch and walked over to the window, peering outside to see if there was anything out there. "I don't see anything, but I definitely hear faint sirens."

They paused to listen for a little longer before Amelia froze. "They aren't so faint anymore, are they?" she asked.

"It does sound like there are getting a bit closer." The two huddled together to see out the window.

"Ohmigosh. They just shut off their sirens and turned the corner onto your street. Do you think they're coming here?"

"I don't see why they would but..." Yvette hesitated and began again, "They might be going to Jamie's house."

"Jamie's house? She lives near here?" Amelia shrieked.

"She's my neighbor. She's living here alone until after the wedding."

"You didn't think to tell me that before we came here to be safe?"

Yvette had thought that the safest place for them was her house. Gavin was right next door, and she wasn't that far from her parent's house, either. After all, she'd expected Heath to have Jamie and Evan meet him at the police station.

"We are safe. The police are here," Yvette joked.

"It's not funny! I'm scared," Amelia exclaimed.

"They just pulled in next door. Let's go outside and see what's going on," she said eagerly.

"Ugh, fine."

Amelia cowered behind Yvette as the two stepped out the front door and onto the porch. Jamie's house was on the other side of Gavin's apartment, so they had to go to that side to see what was going on.

"Shhhh. Look!" Amelia pointed to the house a few moments later.

Yvette looked up to see Heath walk out of the front door followed by Jamie. She was handcuffed and being led down the stairs by another officer but was screaming, "It wasn't me. You have to believe me. I didn't do this!"

"Jamie?" Yvette was stunned.

"Wow. Who would have expected that?" Amelia stepped back.

"Is that Evan?" Amelia asked, noticing someone standing in the doorway of the house.

Yvette nodded. "It's him. Gosh, he must be devasted."

"Let's get inside before Heath sees us snooping," Amelia said. She opened the door and let Yvette in ahead of her.

CHAPTER EIGHTEEN

"I'm still not completely convinced." Yvette sat in her living room, looking between Gavin and Amelia.

"What's there to be unsure of?" Gavin asked. "They obviously arrested Jamie for a reason."

"Something seems off. How would Jamie have even known where to find Jordan? Marissa made it pretty clear that they weren't on good terms, so I doubt she told her where to find him."

"I see what you mean." Amelia nodded. "We have to assume there was evidence that pointed to her though."

"None of it makes sense. Marissa may have said Jordan was a good guy, but I feel like there was more to it than that. He basically tried to ruin Jamie and Evan's wedding."

"Sounds like he dodged a bullet to me, seeing as she killed someone and all." Gavin laughed at his own joke.

"So, you still think Marissa killed her own fiancé?" Amelia asked.

Yvette didn't know what to think, but one way or another she was going to find out. She was going to call Tonya to see if there was any information she might have that could be useful.

"I think I'm going to head into work for a few hours," Yvette told her friends.

Gavin huffed. "Oh, please. Five seconds ago, you were positive that a person was falsely accused of murder and now you want to go to work. We know you better than that."

"I have a gut feeling that I can't ignore, you guys. I'm going to work, but I need to talk to Tonya first. She's not on the schedule today so I'll be going to her house."

"Smart idea telling us where you're going. This way we can call the police if you don't show back up here soon," Amelia said sarcastically.

"You won't be teasing me when I solve this murder." Yvette grabbed her purse and dashed out the door.

Yvette drove mindlessly to Tonya's. She had only been there once before and couldn't remember exactly which house it was. Yvette pulled over to the side of the road to check the contact list in her phone for the address. She put her phone back into her purse and checked her mirrors, making sure nothing was nearby. No matter how secluded the road was, she still wanted to be careful. She stopped when she saw a car coming down the road at full speed. It was heading right for her. The car swerved just in time to miss Yvette's SUV before sliding to a stop and landing in a ditch.

The person in the car hadn't gotten out yet. Before she had too much time to think, she heard female voices screaming in the distance. Yvette looked around but didn't see anyone. She took her keys and phone and slowly opened her car door.

This time she could hear footsteps, almost as if someone was running. The shouting was getting louder.

"Yvette!" Tonya yelled.

"Tonya? Marissa? What's wrong?" Yvette ran to meet the women, not looking back at the car.

"We have to get out of here. You drive." Tonya's chest was rising and falling quickly.

"You need to tell me what's going on first. Do you know who's in the car?" Yvette asked before running around to the driver's side of her SUV.

"It's my Aunt Darla," Marissa blurted. "She came here looking for me and said that if I didn't come with her, something bad was going to happen."

"She's getting out of the car. We have to go now!" Tonya yelled, backing away from Darla.

"But why? Why are we running from her?"

"She just confessed to killing Jordan. My aunt is both reckless and ruthless." Marissa's face was puffy from crying.

"And apparently, dangerous." Yvette's heart raced as they got into the SUV.

Yvette moved her fingers to the ignition but came up emptyhanded. She looked around frantically for her keys.

"What are you doing? Hurry!" Tonya shouted, turning to look out the back window.

"I can't find the keys. I must have dropped them when I got out." Yvette's expression was grim. "If I can just open the door, they might be right outside."

"That's crazy. Let's lock the doors and we can wait for the police. I called them right after Darla left." Tonya was interrupted by a knock on the car door behind her.

Yvette pressed a hand to her chest. "Thank goodness you called them already."

"It's her!" Marissa's jaw dropped. "She has the keys."

"Hey, ladies. I'm so sorry I frightened you." She looked at Yvette. "I seemed to have lost control of my car." Darla's voice was muffled through the closed windows.

"That's the woman who came in Sundae Afternoon the other day." Yvette realized.

Tonya nodded. "I knew she looked familiar, but I only met her once at a family party I went to with Marissa."

"Don't bother." Marissa got out of the car. "You already ruined my wedding and killed my soon-to-be husband. I don't think worrying about telling a lie to a stranger matters very much."

"What is the matter with you? I did you a favor killing him. He was a horrible man," Darla stammered.

"No, he wasn't. He treated me well and the only reason he was so upset was because everyone in my family seemed to only care about Evan's wedding. No one stopped to think about how I felt about everything. I may have agreed to change the date, but you have to know that I didn't want to. Jordan was mad I gave up and let you guys take control of everything. He was only trying to protect me, and you killed him!"

"He tried to ruin my son's wedding. How can you stand here and protect someone like that?"

"The same way you can stand there trying to justify killing your niece's fiancé because he wanted her to have the wedding of her dreams," Marissa yelled, her hands flying around wildly in anger.

Terror took over Marissa's face as Darla took a step closer to her. "I don't care who you are or what you mean to me. No one, and I mean no one, gets in the way of my son's happiness."

"We'll save that for you, Aunt Darla..." Marissa glanced past Darla, noticing the police cruiser headed in their direction. "Nothing like making your son happy by going to prison," she said, glaring at her aunt.

CHAPTER NINETEEN

"Yvette Loretta Lockhart. What were you thinking?!" Her mother stared at her from across the table.

"I know, I know." She hated when her parents used her full name but no matter how old she got, it always achieved the effect they were going for.

Charlie looked at his wife and then glanced toward his daughter. "Call me crazy, but I'm a little proud of her."

"What?" Both women snapped their heads up.

"She was right about nearly everything. If she hadn't realized that Marissa gave the wrong last name, who knows what would have happened? Maybe Yvette has a knack for this sort of thing after all."

"I don't know about all of that, but I'm glad it all

got cleared up. And it shouldn't be too much longer before the lake house is back to normal. I'm sure it'll be quite some time before any of us decide to actually go back up there though," she muttered.

"I can't believe how crazy people get when it comes to weddings," Abigail said, shaking her head slowly.

"No kidding. What I saw up in that loft was gruesome. I know when it comes to love and marriage, some women really take the term bridezilla to a new level. I guess this time it was the mother of the groom who went off her rocker."

Darla had been so upset that Marissa and Jordan had picked the same day for their intimate wedding that she made Evan call and tell them to change it. In turn, Jordan was furious because he knew how much his bride-to-be wanted that date, since it was the day her grandmother was married many years before. Jordan confronted Evan and Darla, telling them it wasn't fair. Marissa said he even went so far as to suggest a double wedding with the people he couldn't stand to be around, just so Marissa could have the wedding she'd hoped for.

After Marissa found out what Jordan did with the caterer, they got into a huge fight. Marissa went to the only place she could think of to find some solace, her family. While Evan and Marissa were trying to come to an agreement, Darla went to the lake house and killed Jordan, then apparently came back to the house, and cooked a full meal and acted like nothing had happened.

"What a shame." Abigail pushed her hair behind her shoulders and slid closer to the table.

"Let's discuss something else." Charlie laughed dryly. "There's something about murder talk at the table that makes me lose my appetite."

Yvette smiled her agreement. "Well, I'll be in Townsend next week, so that's exciting. I'm a little nervous but I'm looking forward to it."

"You'll do great," Charlie told his daughter.

Yvette was thankful to be safe and felt relieved the correct killer had been caught. Jamie was a lovely young woman who was arrested for murder all because Darla called in an anonymous tip offering information that falsely accused her. Darla had ruined the lives of so many people.

When Yvette had spoken with Evan, he'd told her he'd struggle knowing what his mother did, but at the same time, he was thankful that he and his soon-to-be wife could have the wedding they dreamed of, not the one his mother wanted for them.

Yvette had a busy week ahead of her, but she was

happy life was slowly getting back to normal. The first thing she had on her list for the upcoming week was to visit Jerry and his lemonade stand. After all the tragedies Yvette and the town of Heritage had experienced, she knew it was time to bring her old tradition back. Jerry had inspired her to go to the florist weekly and purchase a bouquet to give away as a random act of kindness. Yvette would ask Jerry what he thought about Sundae Afternoon taking a page out of his book and offering tokens as well. He could even keep a few to pass out at his lemonade stand to offer his customers a free ice cream. After all, everyone deserves a little bit of unexpected happiness.

***

If you enjoyed Melt Down Murder and are looking for more Sundae Afternoon adventures, check out A Twist of Murder, today!

AUTHOR'S NOTE

I'd love to hear your thoughts on my books, the storylines, and anything else that you'd like to comment on—reader feedback is very important to me. My contact information, along with some other helpful links, is listed on the next page. If you'd like to be on my list of "folks to contact" with updates, release and sales notifications, etc.… just shoot me an email and let me know. Thanks for reading!

Also…

… if you're looking for more great reads, Summer Prescott Books publishes several popular series by outstanding Cozy Mystery authors.

CONTACT GRETCHEN ALLEN

Visit my website for more information about new releases, upcoming projects, and be sure to check out my special Members Only section for extra freebies and fun!

Website: www.gretchenallen.com

Email: contact@gretchenallen.com

Visit the Summer Prescott Books website to find even more great reads!

Made in United States
North Haven, CT
29 May 2024

53086868R10082